THIS DIARY BELONGS TO

*

Amy

Please return / renew by date shown. Wym/CH
You can renew it at:
norlink.norfolk.gov.uk
or by telephone: 0344 800 8006
Please have your library card & PIN ready

Other titles in the series:

Megan and Mischief
Poppy and Prince
Chloe and Cracker
Sophie and Shine
Charlie and Charm
Emily and Emerald
Lauren and Lucky
Jessica and Jewel
Hannah and Hope
Millie and Magic

www.kellymckain.co.uk

Dear Riders,

A warm welcome to Sunnyside Stables!

Sunnyside is our home and for the next week it will be yours, too! My husband Johnny and I have two children, Millie and James, plus two dogs ... and all the ponies, of course!

We have friendly yard staff and a very talented instructor, Sally, to help you get the most out of your week. If you have any worries or questions about anything at all, just ask. We're here to help, and we want your holiday to be as enjoyable as possible – so don't be shy!

As you know, you will have a pony to look after as your own for the week. Your pony can't wait to meet you and start having fun! During your stay, you'll be caring for your pony, improving your riding, learning new skills and making new friends. Add a beach ride and a gymkhana at the end of the week, and you're in for a fun-packed holiday to remember!

This special Pony Camp Diary is for you to fill with your holiday memories. We hope you'll write all about your adventures here at Sunnyside Stables – because we know you're going to have lots!

Wishing you a wonderful time with us!

Jody xx

Monday morning - quickly scribbling this - we've just arrived

Well, I can't believe we're actually here at last! Me and my best friend Kayla have been saving up for *ages* to come to Pony Camp. Our parents said they'd pay half the money if we earned the other half, so we've been round washing cars for our neighbours and Mum's had me cleaning the bathroom twice a week for the last month!

Me and Kayla have been **BFFs** since reception class and now we're in our final year at Juniors, and we've ridden together most Saturdays for the last two years. Her dad drove us down here (we're from Bromley, near London). My mum and dad, and Kayla's mum are coming to pick us up so they can watch the gymkhana — I can't WAIT for that! But there's so much exciting stuff to do before then — it says in Jody's welcome letter that we're going on a beach ride – how fantastic! I've never been on one before and I'm really excited about cantering along the sand with my pony. I can't believe I'll have my OWN pony – well, for a week anyway! I wonder which one I'll get?! Oh, it's all so brilliant here I feel like I might just BURST like a balloon!

I'm writing this lying on my new bed – I've got the bottom bunk and Kayla's in the one above. She's starting off her diary too. It's great we're sharing a room. We've  unpacked and I've put my video camera in the drawer with my jodhs and T-shirts. Dad gave it to me when he got his new one and I can't wait to start filming our fab holiday adventures!

We've just met Millie and her mum Jody, who'll be looking after us this week. It's Millie's room we're sharing and her bed's over by the window, all messy and covered in cuddlies and mags! She's SO lucky – I wish we lived here all the time too! Jody's given us a timetable of what we'll be doing, which I'll stick in this diary.

Pony Camp Timetable

8am: Wake up, get dressed, have breakfast
8.45am: Help on the yard, bring ponies in from the field, do feeds, etc.
9.30am: Prepare ponies for morning lessons (quick groom, tack up, etc.)
10am: Morning riding lesson
11am: Morning break - drink and biscuits
11.20am: Pony Care talk
12.30pm: Lunch and free time
1.30pm: Prepare ponies for afternoon lesson
2pm: Riding lesson
3pm: Afternoon break - drink and biscuits
3.20pm: Pony Care talk
4.30pm: Jobs around the yard (i.e. cleaning tack, sweeping up, mixing evening feeds, turning out ponies)
5.30pm: Free time before dinner
6pm: Dinner (and clearing up!)
7pm: Evening activity
8.30pm: Showers and hot chocolate
9.30pm: Lights out and NO TALKING!

Kayla read it out and we got so excited
thinking of all the things we'll be
doing that we had to have a
big squealy hug and dance
around the room! A whole
week to spend together,
with our own ponies to
look after, riding every day
and having secret girly chats
every night. Heaven!

Oh, Millie has just stuck her head
round the door and said it's time to
go down to the yard. I feel a bit
nervous about meeting everyone.
Thank goodness me and Kayla came together.

Gotta go — bye!

After lunch

I'm just grabbing a few minutes to write in here before we go back out. I want to get everything down while it's still fresh in my mind and not miss out a single thing!

Well, there was definitely nothing to be nervous about – the other girls are LOVELY! Jody came out to the yard with us and introduced us to Sally, who's the main instructor here, and Lydia, who's the head stable girl.

Then we all had to say our names and where we were from. Sarah, Genevieve and Shanika (all 11) go to the same riding school in London and are sharing a room together.

Sarah Genevieve Shanika

Me, Kayla and Millie are in together of course, so that leaves Jasmine and Lexy (who are BFFs too) and they're sharing with Ava, the youngest. They're all 9, but Ava's only just 9 and Jas is 10 next week.

Lexy Jasmine Ava

Then Sally showed us round the yard. We all went WOW when we saw the swimming pool — it looks even more amazing than in the pics on the Sunnyside Stables website. There's a games room too, with **COOL!** stuff like table tennis and Twister and dance mats.

Next we went into the barn and saw the ponies! They're so gorgeous and my heart was racing with excitement as me and Kayla whispered about which ones we might get! Everyone else felt the same and we made a huge fuss of them all. Back on the yard Sally went through the safety rules about putting equipment away and wearing proper boots and letting an adult know if we leave the group to go to the loo or anything.

Then came the bit we'd all been waiting for — finding out which ponies we were getting! Lydia brought them out one by one and Sally paired us up. This is who everyone got:

Sunnyside Stables

Sarah + Charm

Genevieve + Shine

Millie + Magic
(her own pony – lucky thing!)

Shanika + Jewel

Jasmine + Sugar

Lexy + Monsoon

Me + AMBER!!!

Ava + Star

Kayla + Cracker
(a cute, cheeky little grey)

Sunnyside Stables

Amber is SO gorgeous! Here's my pony profile of her:

Name: Amber

Height: 13hh

Age: 6

Breed: Maybe some New Forest pony in her, Lydia thinks!

Colour: Dun

Markings: White star, dark brown mane and tail and a cute blackish-brown line down her back

Fave foods: Carrots and apples (according to Millie)

Personality: Sweet, patient, tries hard and GORGEOUS!!

We all lined up to use the mounting block and once we were on, Sally and Lydia came round to sort out our stirrups and girths. Amber was so sweet and stood really quietly so I didn't need any help, but Sally had to hold Cracker because he kept wandering off whenever Kayla tried to put her leg forward.

We rode into the manège in single file and my heart was pounding because I wanted to impress Sally. As we were walking around to warm up I kept thinking too much about my posture and hands and legs and I felt really awkward, but after a while I relaxed into it. I so enjoyed riding Amber, she makes lovely smooth transitions and she always stopped nice and square when we went forward into halt.

Kayla's pony Cracker is so cute and cheeky. He cut off the corner when we had to trot to the back of the ride, and Sally got her to circle him round and do it again twice. He kept to the track after that, and Sally said Kayla had done really well.

And guess what?! She did *so* well that she's been put in Group B with Shanika, Sarah, Genevieve and Millie. (I'm in Group A with Lexy, Jas and Ava, which is fine by me!) I thought Kayla would be really happy, but when we were untacking in the barn afterwards she was a bit upset that we won't be riding together. She even wanted me to go with her to ask Sally if she could swap to Group A.

I was secretly a bit upset too, because of course I'd wanted us to ride together, but I was careful to hide it. There's no way I'd hold her back – that's not what good friends do. "You should be proud that you got into the top group," I told her. "You're such a good rider. This is a great chance to really push yourself."

Kayla looked uncertain. "Do you really think so?" she asked.

"Of course I do! Go for it!" I cried, giving her
a big hug. "And don't forget,

BIG HUG!

we'll still have our hack out
and beach ride together."
Kayla shrugged, then
smiled. "OK."

It was great fun brushing our ponies down
next to each other and getting them some fresh
water and checking their hooves and everything.

Oh, Millie's just come in and said it's time to
go back down to the yard again. Gotta go —
I can't wait one more second to see Amber!
I know I've only just met her, but I'm completely
crazy about her already!

Amber

I'm in bed! It's the first chance I've had to write in here since lunch!

Right now, me, Kayla and Millie are waiting till Jody's gone to bed so we can have our first midnight feast (there's no way we can wait till actual midnight!). So in the meantime I'm writing this under the covers by the light of my torch.

Wow – there's so much to say! Loads has happened. I'll go back to when we went down to the yard after lunch, so I don't miss anything out. Well, first we had a talk about tack and tacking up, and after Lydia had given us a demo on Charm, we all had a go with our own ponies. Amber stood really still while I brushed her down and got her saddle and bridle on.

Good girl!

Cheeky boy! Then I had to help Kayla get the bit in as Cracker kept tossing his head around whenever she tried.

Our lesson was really fun. There are two manèges next to each other, so both groups ride at the same time. Group B had Sally and we had Jody. She got us doing lots of balancing exercises like riding without stirrups and doing Round the Worlds. I loved it and I know Amber did too. And she was so sweet putting up with me bobbling about at first when we had to trot without stirrups! Jody told us to sit deep in our saddles and let our legs wrap lightly round our ponies, and soon I had a much more secure seat (which was good 'cos otherwise I would have ended up with a v. v. sore bottie!).

Next we had to canter round the manège (*with* stirrups – phew!) then ride a 20-metre circle at the far end. That was amazing!

OK, so some of our circles were a bit egg-shaped, including mine, but Jody told us it didn't matter. She said that by the end of the week we'd have perfect ones. She's so nice and patient, I'm really glad I'm in her group. I told Kayla about it afterwards while we were brushing our ponies down and getting them fresh water. She didn't say much about her lesson (probably because she couldn't get a word in edgeways, poor thing!) and I was just about to ask when Lydia came in and gave us our yard jobs.

I was in charge of sweeping the yard with Lexy and we got really into it. We even chased the last little bits of straw around in the wind before they reached the ground to make sure there was not one speck of mess! Then Sally came out of the office to see our work. She said how fab it was and how she'd give us jobs at Sunnyside if we were old enough!

When we'd all finished, we gathered in the barn with Lydia to turn out our ponies. That's when I suddenly remembered my video camera, and I asked Lydia if I could run back to the farmhouse and fetch it. I wanted to get some film of Amber and the other ponies just hanging out in the field. And I'm so glad I did, because it was just fantastic! Amber did a big roll and then went flying about with Charm, both of them kicking their heels and whinnying.

Cute!

And even more amazing was what happened afterwards at teatime…

We were all sitting round the big table in the kitchen of the farmhouse chatting about our first day, and eating our jacket potatoes and salad and chicken. You could just help yourself to what you wanted, and I ate THREE drumsticks 'cos I was so hungry after all the riding! Jody put my camera up on a shelf so it didn't get covered in food and only gave it back after our pud (banana splits – YUM!).

All the girls wanted to see what I'd filmed, so I showed them on the little monitor. They all went "Aww!" when Amber did the roll, and Jody said it was really good. Then she said something amazing which was, "Would you make us a film to go on our website showing how much fun it is at Sunnyside Stables?"

Well, WOW!!!

I said YES, of course! Everyone instantly started coming up with loads of ideas about what could be in it, like demos of jumping and flatwork, us all out on a hack and riding on the beach, going swimming, the yummy meals, the end of week disco and the gymkhana. The only problem was they were all talking at once!

"Hang on! Hang on!" I cried. "One at a time!"

Jody found me a piece of paper and a pen so I could make a list. As well as the girls' ideas, I'm going to film us doing yard work and looking after our ponies too – to show that coming on holiday here really *is* like having one of your own!

Jody even said we can run the lessons on a bit on Wednesday so that I can film Group B jumping (we can't do it tomorrow 'cos it's meant to be really hot and sunny so they've moved the beach ride forward by a day – hooray!).

Our group is going to do a flatwork demo then too. Jody said she'd ask James (Millie's bro) to film it so that I can join in – how cool!

Me and Kayla had planned to go upstairs after tea and listen to my iPod together, but by the time we'd all finished talking about everyone's ideas we just had to hurry up and get changed to go swimming. I grabbed my camera, so I could make a start on the film right there and then!

When we were at the pool, Lexy had a fab idea for me to film them all jumping in one after the other. They each tried to make the biggest splash and it looked brilliant!
Then it was really funny
'cos they were all
chanting my name so I
gave my camera to Jody
to look after and did a big
jump into the middle!

It's so great here, I'm having the most fantastic time EVER! The girls are lovely and it's been easy to make friends, and best of all I've got my perfect pony! It's exactly what me and Kayla have been dreaming about for weeks! I can't believe the first day's over already – it feels like our time here is going way too fast! I can't wait for

Tuesday - we're off in a minute!

Whoops, I nodded off while I was writing in here last night! Kayla tried to wake me and Millie up so we could have our midnight feast, but we were so fast asleep she had to give up in the end! It's a beautiful day for the beach ride, and Jody says it's going to be hot, hot, hot!

It was brilliant going up to the field to get Amber this morning. I loved walking up the lane with the other girls, all of us laughing and chatting, with head collars over our shoulders. Amber let me catch her straight away and I gave her a big pat and told her what a good girl she is.

Back in the barn, Sally explained that not all the ponies can come to the beach because there's not enough room in the horsebox, so

we have to share. Amber's coming, though —
hooray! Sally's bringing her horse Blue, so she
can ride along with us for safety, and Sarah's
going to share Charm with James, who's coming
along for the trip too. Shanika's sharing Jewel
with Genevieve, Jasmine's got Magic with Millie,
Lexy's sharing Monsoon with Ava, and I'm
sharing Amber with Kayla. I think she was a bit
sad for a while that Cracker wasn't coming, but
everyone was so excited about the beach ride
she soon got swept up in it too. And after a
talk from Lydia about leg and tail bandaging (to
protect against knocks during journeys) we all
got to practise on our own ponies, so Kayla had
a bit of extra time with Cracker.

Jody and Sally are coming in
the minibus with us (Sally's
driving) and James is going in
the Land Rover with Johnny.
It's a private beach a friend of

30

Jody's owns so that's why we're allowed to ride on it. How amazing – imagine having your own *beach*!

We've got all our stuff packed and Jody's reminded us about a million times to bring our sun cream, like my mum does whenever we go anywhere!

Sally's just come in and said the ponies are all loaded up and it's time to go!

Tuesday, hanging out in the kitchen after tea

We're all really tired now so we're just sitting here writing our diaries. The beach ride was BRILLIANT!!! I honestly think it was the best day of my life so far!

When we arrived we all got out of the minibus and stood back while the adults unloaded the ponies. The beach looked beautiful in the sunshine with the waves crashing on the shore. Then we took off the bandages and tacked up, all giggling and chatting, and led them down over the powdery sand to the firmer bit near the sea.

The people who were borrowing ponies got to ride first, so that was James, Genevieve, Jasmine, Ava and Kayla, of course. I gave her a leg up on to Amber and sorted out her stirrups

for her, and then they were off. I'd wanted Sally
to take my camera with her and film them as
she was riding along, but she said that might be
a bit dangerous. So in the end I showed them
going off up the beach into the distance. Then
about twenty minutes later they reappeared and
I got some fab shots of them trotting back
towards us. The ponies' legs were wet – they'd
been in the sea as well! I couldn't WAIT to ride
when I saw that!

Kayla was grinning from ear to ear when she
came back. "I loved riding Amber," she cried.
"I mean, I love Cracker too, of course, but she's

so much easier to handle. She just did what I asked with no fuss and she really enjoyed being out in the open!"

"That's great!" I said, and we both gave Amber a big pat for being so good.

The ponies had a drink and a little break, then Sally said, "Come on, girls, let's get going before we melt!" I wanted Kayla to take over with my camera, but she wasn't confident about using it, so James filmed our group instead.

Riding Amber on the beach was amazing! First we walked along to get used to the feeling of being on sand and then we moved up into trot. And then, fabbiest of all, we had a canter! It was brilliant thundering along the sand, just like being in a movie!

Then we slowed up and had lots of fun splashing in the waves, which Amber loved. Charm wasn't that keen on getting his feet wet at first, but with a bit of encouragement from Sarah he was soon prancing about like everyone else. Lexy lost her seat at one point and she was just hanging sideways off Monsoon, desperately trying to pull herself back into the saddle before she plopped into the water.

Poor Lexy!

The problem was, she was giggling so much she didn't have any strength in her arms! We were all laughing too and we gave her a big cheer when she finally made it up!

Sally had the great idea of giving James an action shot, so we came thundering back towards the group at full gallop! I watched the footage on the monitor afterwards and it looks amazing – it's really going to make the film extra-fantastic.

We were SO hot after that and the second our feet touched the sand we all pulled off our hats (everyone's hair was soaked with sweat — yuck!). We just wanted to get changed and jump into the waves, but of course we had to see to our ponies first. So we led them back up to the horsebox, untacked them and gave them a quick brush down with our partners' help.

Then we tied them up along the shady side of the horsebox with some fresh water and hay nets to munch on. And I gave Amber another big hug for being such a star!

There was no stopping us after that! We all went to change into our swimming stuff in the horsebox and there was loads of giggling because we kept sending each other to the doors at the back to make sure James wasn't looking! We ran out into the sea (after Jody had made us cover ourselves in even *more* sun cream, that is!). The grown-ups all had their swimming stuff with them too, so they got changed and came in with us!

The lovely cool water was so refreshing after the hot ride, and we had fun jumping over the waves and trying to lift each other up out of the water! Then Johnny went to look after the ponies and James came crashing into the sea. Sarah and Genevieve were giggling loads and whispering to each other – I think they've got *crushes* on him. Yuck! Back on the beach we all dried off and put on even *more* sun cream!

And guess what…

There was Johnny lining up disposable barbecues next to the Land Rover. What a brilliant surprise! No one had said anything

Yum!

about a beach barbie – I'd thought it would just be sarnies! Anyway, I was so hungry after all the riding and swimming I ate two hotdogs, two vegetable kebabs and a whole sweetcorn!

I thought *everyone* was having a fab time, but while we were all sitting on our towels eating, Kayla seemed a bit weird with me, like she was in a mood or something. When I asked what was wrong, she just shrugged. Then she sighed and said, "I don't know. I suppose I wish Cracker had come on the trip, that's all."

I frowned. "But you loved riding Amber, didn't you?"

"Yeah," she sighed, "it's just, it would have been nice to be in the galloping shot with you, for the film. At this rate, we won't have *any* footage of us riding together."

"But we couldn't both ride the same pony at once, could we?" I replied.

Kayla gave me a frustrated look, like I wasn't getting it, which I suppose I wasn't. I mean, the ride wasn't that long, and I was just concentrating on what I was doing, and having fun with Amber. Why couldn't Kayla do the same? It was no big deal. Just then, Jody asked me to go round with a bin bag and collect up the paper plates, so we didn't say any more about it. It was strange, though.

After the clearing up was done, we were all hanging out, sunbathing and reading the mags that we'd brought and passing them round. Shanika had us all in stitches reading out the "Readers' Fess Ups" from *Pony* mag.

Tee hee!

Later on, Johnny set up a net and we had a game of beach volleyball. I've never played it before but it was really good, especially because you can just throw yourself on to the sand to reach the ball and it doesn't hurt at all! I got some great film of us playing, too!

When it was time to pack up, none of us wanted to come back. But then Jody said if we got a move on there'd be time for us to give the beach ride ponies a brush and turn them out before tea (she said the others had been turned out already so they could spend the day playing in the field). So, of course, everyone hurried up into the minibus then.

Even that was really fun because
we sang songs all the way
back. Shanika and Sarah have
got really good voices – they
were doing harmonies and everything!

Hey, guess what? Now Jody's making us
some chocolate brownies to go with our hot
choc! Double choc – yummy!

Wednesday, just after lunch.
Kayla's in a mood with me and
I don't even know why!

She didn't sit with me at lunch just now
and I'm not going over to *her*. After all, she's the
one who shouted at me in the barn and who's
in a strop for no reason. I'm just going to get on
with my diary and ignore her!

This morning we had a talk about grooming
and then we had to do a head to toe groom
on our own ponies, as Lydia had shown us.
It was really fun, like a pony spa, and I got
Genevieve and Sarah on film
pretending to be beauty
therapists!
Genevieve was saying
things to Shine like, "So,
madam, are you going
anywhere nice on your holidays?"

and Sarah was asking Charm if he'd thought of having some auburn lowlights in his mane to bring out the colour of his eyes. Everyone was in stitches and I was laughing so much there was a lot of shake on the camera, but never mind! It'll be great to have some bits in the film which show how much fun it is just hanging out with our ponies.

I gave Amber a really good groom with the rubber curry comb, making circles as Lydia had shown us. It got the oils in her coat to the surface so she looked really, really shiny. Then I finished off with some nice long strokes from the body brush. I could tell she was really enjoying it – it must be like having a massage!

Kayla didn't seem her normal self, though. I mean, I started off chatting a few times and she didn't say anything back so I gave up. At first I thought she was just concentrating really hard on getting all the bits of dried mud off Cracker's legs, but then when I asked her to film a bit of me grooming Amber she *snapped* at me!

"Oh, it's all about the film, isn't it?" she said stroppily. "You're so wrapped up in it. And so much for having our midnight feast last night!"

"It's not my fault I fell asleep again," I said. "I was really tired after the beach ride."

"It's not just that — it's everything! It's *you*, Amy!" she shouted, then stormed off.

I mean — WHAT?!

Where did that come from?

Lydia was across in the far pen so she hadn't heard, but some of the girls had.

"Are you OK?" Shanika asked, ducking under

Jewel's lead rope and coming to put her arm round me.

I nodded, but I felt a bit shocked, to be honest.

Lexy frowned. "What's up with her? That was a bit over the top."

"Shall I go and see where she's got to?" asked Jas. "We're supposed to stick together."

I shrugged. I thought maybe *I* should go after Kayla, but I didn't feel like it. Not after she'd shouted at me for no reason.

Anyway, no one went to find her in the end because Sally came in to say it was lesson time and Kayla crept in behind her and slipped back into our pen. I tried to catch her eye, but she wouldn't even look at me. Well, fine if she wants to be like that.

Luckily, our lesson was so good, and Amber

was so brilliant and such a star, that I managed
to forget about what had happened with Kayla.
Afterwards, us Group A girls quickly led our
ponies back into the barn and untacked. Then
we came out to the manège again. The plan
was for me to film the Group B girls jumping,
and the rest of my group came along to watch.
We all sat up on the viewing gallery where I
could get some really good shots.

Sally had set up a mini jumping course, with

a double up the long side, then
a single on the diagonal and
a change of rein and canter
lead to get them round to a
bounce up the other long side.

I tried not to let falling out with Kayla affect me,
and kept smiling and telling the girls what a
great job they were doing and how fab it
looked. And it really did – especially when
Genevieve got Shine to do a flying change

instead of bringing her back into trot to change canter lead! Sarah flew round on Charm, and Millie and Magic were fantastic as well — they're such a great team it's hard to believe it's only their second week together.

When Shanika forgot to steer Jewel round to the fence on the diagonal and ended up popping the bounce from the wrong direction, we all burst out laughing, including her! Then, last of all, it was Kayla's turn. She jumped the double well, but didn't get into the corner enough before the diagonal. She approached it at a funny angle and Cracker had the pole down with a back leg, then stumbled a bit to keep his balance. This unseated Kayla and she came flying off.

She got up straight away, but – YUCK – she'd landed in a pile of poo that Charm had just done and there was a long smear of it down her jodhs!

We all did this kind of cheering and clapping thing, like you do when someone drops a plate in the dining hall at school, and I thought Kayla would grin and take a bow or something. But instead she went bright red and shouted, "There's no way you're using that bit in the film, Amy!"

"Oh, come on! Don't be a spoilsport," Lexy cried. "It's hilarious!"

"Yeah, that was classic!" added Jas. "You should write into 'Readers' Fess Ups'! That was easily as funny as the ones they print in the mag!"

"No way," snapped Kayla. "I am not having *her* make me look like an idiot!" She gave me a very moody glare then, and Sally stepped in, saying, "Kayla, calm down." Then she turned to the Group B girls. "Right, on that note I think we'll get back to the yard. Well done, everyone, I'm sure there'll be some excellent footage for the video."

So they walked their ponies back in and us Group A girls followed along, chatting as usual, but the way Kayla was acting had taken the shine off things, to be honest. I mean, she only fell in a bit of poo. Once I stepped backwards into a whole wheelbarrow of it at the stables where we ride and we both laughed so much our cheeks hurt! I don't know why she had to take it so seriously today. Or why she said "*her*" in that horrible way, to mean me.

She didn't speak to me in the barn while we were mucking out the pens, so I just ignored her back and filmed Jas and Lexy instead. They were pretending to nearly faint because of the smell as they loaded the old straw into the wheelbarrow.

It was funny, but at the same time it made me feel even sadder because me and Kayla should have been messing about like that, too. We've been looking forward to this holiday for so long and now we're here I don't understand why she's spoiling it.

Anyway, Amber looked so cute tied up outside the pen munching hay that I set the camera up on a couple of straw bales to film her. Then I got on with mucking out. Oh, I've just realized, I must have left it behind when we got called in for lunch. We're going out to the yard in about half an hour, when the clearing up's all done, but I'll ask Jody if I can quickly pop out and get it now.

Wednesday, before tea.
What an afternoon!

Well, I hurried back out to the barn and...

My camera wasn't there!

It wasn't on the bales where I'd left it, and I looked and looked but I couldn't see it anywhere. I just stood there, not knowing what to do, with my heart banging and my stomach churning.

Where on earth was it?

All my footage for the video was gone! And what would Dad say about me losing the camera?

I ran back to the farmhouse and blurted out to everyone that it was missing. I felt really panicky, and the others just looked shocked.

"All your hard work!" Jas cried.

"What are we going to do about the video?" Lexy asked.

Jody gave me a big hug. "Now, let's not

panic," she said calmly. "It has to be
around here somewhere. Are you
sure you left it in the barn? You
didn't bring it in here with you and
put it down?"

I shook my head. "I put it on the
straw bales to film Amber while we were
mucking out the pens," I told her.

That's when I felt a shiver run down my
spine. I looked at Jody. She was thinking the
same thing. "Could it have fallen into the straw
and been taken out to the muck heap?" she
asked.

"Maybe," I murmured.

"OK, who wants to help Amy look for it?"
she said. It was so nice that all the girls
volunteered, even Kayla. "Right, Millie, Kayla and
Shanika, you go with Amy and check the muck
heap. Sarah and Genevieve, you go and look in

the barn again. Jas, Lexy and Ava, you're on the rota for clearing up so you can help search as soon as you've finished, OK? Although I'm sure you'll have found it by then, Amy," she added, giving me a smile.

Everyone went out into the porch bit and started pulling their boots on. I did too, but then I suddenly needed the loo, and when I came out, Kayla was there alone, waiting for me.

"Amy, I need to say something..." she began, looking sheepish. She blushed. "Well, it's, I..."

Just then, Shanika and Millie poked their heads back in. They looked at me looking at Kayla. "What is it?" I asked her, impatient to get outside.

"I'm really sorry for being horrible to you this morning," she gabbled. "I was just being silly. Can you forgive me?"

Maybe in another situation I would have
asked her why she'd acted like that. But I was
just glad she was back to her usual self, and I
wanted to get on with finding the camera, so I
said, "Yeah, course, come on, let's go."

She linked arms with me. "Don't worry, we'll
find it and everything will be OK," she said.

"That's right," added Millie. Shanika linked
arms with me on the other side and out
we went.

Well, we searched the muck heap for what
felt like ages, turning over the
straw with forks. We had
to stand right ON the
pile and it really
smelled. There was no
sign of the camera and I got
that heart-hammering feeling again, especially
when Sarah and Genevieve came back and said
there was no sign in the barn either. Then Jas,

Sunnyside Stables

Lexy and Ava came out and asked what they could do to help. "I don't know," I gasped, feeling my eyes prickle with tears. "It's not anywhere here!"

Sally came over to us then, looking very serious. "Sorry to hear about your camera, Amy," she said, frowning. "It hasn't been handed in to the office and I've asked all the staff – no one's picked it up. And Jody's double-checked the farmhouse. I'm afraid we have to consider the possibility that it's been stolen, and if so then this is a very serious matter indeed."

We all gasped. *Stolen?* No one had even *thought* of that. I mean, who would do something so terrible?!

"Anyway, I'm sure that's not the case, and it'll turn up soon," Sally said then, seeing the startled look on my face. "Right, we really must get ready for the lesson now, girls."

"What about our riding display for the video?" I asked.

"Yeah, we've planned it all out and everything," added Jas.

This morning in our lesson we'd come up with this whole flatwork routine to film. Seeing how disappointed everyone was just made me feel even more awful and that was the final straw. I couldn't hold the tears back any more and I burst into loud sobs.

Kayla hugged me, and then Shanika and Millie did too. "Hey, don't worry," said Kayla, "Like Sally says, it'll turn up."

We started to walk back towards the yard to get our tack. On our way down the lane Kayla stopped by the grass verge. "Oh, I think I've got a stone in my boot," she said, frowning. "You all go on,

I'll just stop here and sort it out."

Usually, I would have waited for her, but Sally was calling us to hurry up, so I carried on with the others. But we'd only gone a few paces when...

"Hey!" called Kayla. "Look, it's here!"

She was crouching in a patch of long grass by the side of the lane. Then she held up my camera! I ran back and gave her a big hug. "Oh, Kayla, well done! You star!" I cried. It was such a relief to have the camera there, in my hand. I kept looking down at it and grinning.

"It was just here, it must have fallen out of a barrow on the way to the muck heap," Kayla said. "When I took my boot off, I thought I saw a flash of silver in the grass. I went over to have a look and there it was!"

"We've found it!" Millie yelled across the lane. The others all clapped and cheered.

"Well done!" cried Sarah, as we caught them up. "We should have thought to look all along the route as well!"

"I've got it back, that's all that matters," I told her. "And thanks for helping, everyone. I really thought it was gone..." I had to stop myself from bursting into tears again then – tears of relief this time!

So, my group had another cool lesson and we were really excited that we'd get to do the riding demo after all. In fact, Jody said we were all a bit *too* excited, and told us off a few times for getting giggly and messing about! In the end she made us do loads of changes of pace and rein and turns and circles, and kept us going for ages and ages so we *had* to calm down and

concentrate or we would have all crashed into
each other!

The riding demo went really well too. It
looked so cool when we went on different
reins and did figures of eight weaving in
between each other, as if the ponies were
dancing. Finally, we each cantered to the back
of the ride and then all turned in off the track,
halted facing James and bowed to the camera!

Group B were watching too, and they gave
us a big clap and cheer at the end. I was really
pleased with how it had gone and I made a big
fuss of Amber for doing so well.

Afterwards we had a talk about feeding, then we got to make up all the evening feeds for the ponies and horses, mixing the ingredients like in a recipe. Each feed was different and we had to concentrate. Sally kept an eye on us and stopped Kayla just in time when she was about to add a scoopful of oats to Cracker's bucket by accident (it was supposed to be for Jody's horse Bella, next on the chart!).

"I wouldn't give him that," she joked. "Or he'll be even more of a crazy Cracker than ever!"

CRAZY CRACKER We all laughed, including Kayla, and it was so good to be happy together with no moods going on.

Just now at teatime we were all chatting together too, telling stories about our fave and worst riding moments. And of course we told Jody exactly how Kayla found the camera, and she said a big well done and got everyone to give her a clap, which made her blush!

We're off to play rounders in the lower field now and then we're going to watch all the footage I've got so far for the video. Everyone's desperate to see themselves on film and Jody's going to make us some popcorn to go with it too!

Wednesday - after lights out, writing this in bed by torchlight

I still can't believe what's happened. What a shock!

Well, when we came in from rounders, we all got some squash and settled down in the little TV room, munching popcorn. The girls squealed when they saw themselves on camera and went "Aw!" every time the ponies did something cute! The beach ride shots and Group B jumping looked especially cool (but I fast forwarded the bit of Kayla falling in the poo so she didn't get upset again).

Then we came to the bits I'd taken this morning in the barn and I realized that of course the camera had still been filming when I left it on the hay bales. "We'll see it drop into the straw in a minute," I said to the other girls, "and then me sweeping it up and putting it into the wheelbarrow."

Then the picture went funny as someone accidentally nudged the bales making the camera fall, just as I'd guessed.

Lexy gasped. "Ooohh, we're going to get a poo's eye view in a minute!"

But as we watched, I didn't see myself sweep it up into a wheelbarrow. Instead, Lydia said it was time for us to go in for lunch, and the camera kept filming as we packed away the mucking out stuff and checked our ponies' pens for stray hoof picks or head collars before leading them back in.

You could hear someone swishing through

the straw of our pen, then saying "Oh!" as she came into view above the camera.

It was *Kayla*.

She picked it up and turned it off, and that's the last thing we saw.

I stared at her. I felt like I'd swallowed a brick. "But ... you had it all along!" I croaked.

All the girls were looking shocked and confused. "Why didn't you give it straight back to Amy?" Millie demanded.

That's what I was wondering.

Kayla had gone bright red. "I ... well ... it's just ... I..." she stammered.

Before I knew it, I found myself running out of the farmhouse and up to the field. I know we aren't supposed to go off on our own, but I didn't even think about that at the time. I just wanted to be with Amber.

As soon as she saw me she came trotting
up to the fence. I climbed into the
field, flung my arms round her
neck and burst into tears. "The
camera *was* stolen!" I wailed. "By
my own so-called best friend!"

Amber whinnied gently and nuzzled into me.

"How could she?" I sobbed. I couldn't say
anything else because I was crying too much
by then.

Amber snorted and nuzzled my shoulder
again and I clung to her even more tightly.

Millie found us a few minutes later. "Are you
OK?" she asked.

I just shrugged and hugged Amber tighter.

"Erm, sorry, but Mum says you have to
come back in," she said gently. "Kayla wants to
talk to you."

"Well, I don't want to talk to *her*," I sniffled.

But I knew I had to go in or Jody would be

cross, so I gave Amber one last squeeze and climbed back over the fence. Millie didn't say anything else, she just put her arm round me and together we trudged back down the lane.

The second I stepped into the kitchen, Kayla started talking. "Amy, listen, it's not how it looks," she cried. "Please, you've got to believe me. I never meant to keep the camera from you."

I glared at her. "Well, why did you then?"

The others must have still been in the TV room, because Millie hurried off in that direction. Only Jody was there, standing by the sink with her arms folded, *not* looking very happy. "I'd like to hear your explanation, Kayla, and I'm sure Amy would too," she said sternly.

"Well?" I demanded.

"I meant to give it to you as soon as I got in for lunch," Kayla insisted, "but you weren't here. I thought you were probably washing your hands upstairs or something, and I was about to go up too, but then Jody asked me to set the table. By the time you came down, all the others were here and honestly, it just slipped my mind. It was only after lunch when you found out it was missing that I remembered."

"But why didn't you just give it to me then?" I demanded.

Kayla glanced nervously at Jody. Then she sighed. "I know I should have done. But I panicked. I'd been so moody with you this morning, in front of everyone, I was worried you'd all think I'd taken it on purpose, just to be horrible. I did try to tell you the truth, when you came out of the loo, but then Millie and Shanika appeared. I was just so scared that if everyone thought I'd stolen it, I'd be in massive trouble and get sent home. Even worse, I thought you'd hate me and stop being friends with me. I didn't know what to do then, so when we went out to search I hid it in the long grass on the way. I thought someone would soon find it, but no one thought to look along the track between the barn and the muck heap. In the end I realized I had to 'find' it myself."

"But you saw how upset I was!" I cried. "I thought I'd lost all the footage for the video, *and* the camera!"

"I'm so sorry," she wailed. "I never meant to hurt you – I was just so scared that I ended up doing something stupid. Please, Amy, you have to believe me. I didn't take it on purpose, I would never, ever do something like that."

I sighed. "I know," I told her. "But you could have just told me the truth. We're supposed to be BFFs after all."

Jody gave me a smile. "Well, I'll leave you girls to it," she said gently, slipping out of the room.

I was really surprised then, because Kayla burst into tears. "It hasn't felt like we are," she sniffled. "I've been feeling so lonely over the past few days. I wanted us to ride together, but when I got put in another group you didn't even seem bothered."

"Course I was bothered!" I gasped. "But I was trying to be a good friend! Being in Group B was such a great opportunity for you. I knew it would be selfish of me to hold you back."

"But I didn't care about getting to do more in lessons!" she insisted. "What I'd been looking forward to most about this holiday was us two having fun together. But you didn't seem to care about that so I thought I may as well go in Group B."

I felt really bad then for not realizing that.

"And the truth is, I've been struggling in that group," Kayla mumbled, blushing. "I can't get Cracker to do what I want like the other girls can with their ponies. I know Sally thinks I'm rubbish."

I blinked at her, totally shocked. There I was thinking we were having the best week of our lives, and instead she was miserable! "Why didn't you talk to me about this?" I asked, more gently.

"I wanted to, on the beach," she told me. "But I didn't know what to say. And I should have tried again this morning, instead of just getting into a state. I'm so sorry, Amy."

"It's me who should be saying sorry," I insisted.

"Well, OK, maybe it's both of us," said Kayla. She smiled at me, wiping her eyes, and I smiled back. I still feel guilty about how wrapped up I've been — I mean, how could I not have even noticed that she wasn't enjoying herself?

"Things will be different from
now on," I promised her.
I gave her a big hug, and
she hugged me back.
"I suppose we should go and
face the others," I said then.

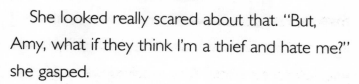

She looked really scared about that. "But,
Amy, what if they think I'm a thief and hate me?"
she gasped.

"It'll be OK," I said, squeezing her hand. "We'll
explain what happened. They'll understand."

She didn't seem very sure, and neither was I
to be honest, but we went into the TV room
anyway. We explained what had happened and
Kayla apologized to everyone a LOT for not
giving me the camera straight away. They were
pretty moody about it, and Shanika was
annoyed that she'd had to search through the
muck heap for no reason. I could see how
much that upset Kayla and I squeezed her hand.

Then Jody sent everyone upstairs to have
their showers, but us two hung
behind. And, with a lot of
encouragement from me,
Kayla told her about
struggling in Group B.
Jody was really nice about it
(phew!) and she's going to have a
chat with Sally tomorrow morning.

She also had the idea that we should think of
something to do for the film, so that we'll have
some shots of us two together after all. We
both thought that was a good idea and we're
going to come up with something. That seemed
to cheer Kayla up a bit, and when we came
down in our PJs for hot chocolate the other
girls gradually started chatting to her again, so
that was a big relief, for both of us.

Well, I'm totally shattered now. Not too
tired for a midnight feast though! It's all quiet

now, and Jody and Johnny have gone into their
sitting room. I'm just going to give Kayla the
secret signal to sneak down to my bunk, and
then see if Millie wants to join in too.

Thursday after lunch

It's absolutely bucketing down (what a change from Tuesday!), so Jody suggested we stay put for a while and catch up on our diaries instead of heading straight down to the yard to do jobs. It's really cool 'cos we're all sitting round the kitchen table together sharing our glitter gel pens and things.

Our midnight feast (well, 10.21 p.m. feast!) was really fun. We tried to get Millie to join in but she was fast asleep, so it was just us two. We hung our towels down from the top bunk to hide our torchlight and we had to remember to whisper. We kept clamping our hands over our mouths every time a giggle came out, but that just made us laugh even more! We chatted for hours − and I can't believe we scoffed that whole big packet of cola bottles!

This morning when we were in the barn brushing our ponies down, Sally came and had a chat with Kayla. She was really nice, luckily – Kayla had been worried she'd be cross. "I actually think you're doing really well," Sally told her. "Cracker's not the easiest pony, and you've made a lot of progress with him."

Kayla gaped at her. "You honestly think I'm doing OK?" she asked.

"Yes, brilliantly," Sally promised her. "And I'm sorry if that hasn't come across. You should have confidence in yourself. But saying that, I'll leave it up to you which group you'd like to be in for the rest of the week. We just want you to be happy here and have fun."

Kayla looked at me and I gave her an encouraging smile. "I'd like to stay in Group B, please," she told Sally. Good for her!

After our lessons, when we were untacking in the barn, Kayla was really excited because they'd had a go at dressage and she'd managed to get Cracker to go from walk straight to canter! So she definitely made the right choice! I know I'm not ready for that sort of thing myself just yet, but I was SO pleased for her.

We had loads of fun in our lesson as well — we did some jumping today, first working over trotting poles and then a small cross pole before trying an upright. Amber just loved it, and she was so steady I even managed to clamber back up when I lost my seat on my second go and nearly came off!

I love being here and it's fantastic that Kayla's enjoying herself so much more too. It's just going to be fun, fun and more fun for us two from now on, starting this afternoon... If we ever get out of here, that is! We're supposed to be having our hack, but we probably won't be able to go out if it carries on pouring down.

Oh, Sally's just come in and said we can skip yard work altogether and have our Pony Care talk in the barn now and then see what happens with the weather, so gotta go!

We've got some free time before tea, which we're using to dry off and catch up on our diaries.

Where was I? Oh, yes, Sally called us into the barn to have our Pony Care talk first, because of the rain. It was so cool being in there because we could hear it absolutely pelting down on the roof, but we were all cosy and warm squashed up together on the hay bales.

When Lydia talked about the points of the horse and conformation, she used my lovely Amber to demonstrate on! Of course, she stood really nicely, and I gave her a big pat afterwards for doing so well.

Then we got sheets to fill in, and we had to look at all the ponies in the barn and see how many different colours and markings we could find. I went round with Kayla and we found loads. By the end the rain had eased off – only

a bit, but Sally said we could go on the hack —
hooray! I dashed back into the farmhouse and
grabbed my camera, tucking it into the pocket
of my wax jacket to keep it dry.

The hack was fantastic and we didn't care at
all that we were getting SOAKED. Sally rode
at the front and Lydia at the back, with the
rest of us in single file in between. Everything
was really green and fresh, and Amber loved
being out in the open.

Kayla was a bit nervous at first about
Cracker bolting off because he kept going into
trot and breaking out of the line, but Sally
moved them to be behind Ava and Star (who
is really chilled out), and showed her how to
keep her outside leg on and use the reins so
he stayed put. As we turned into this beautiful
lane at the edge of a field, the rain stopped,
and a bit later the sun came out and guess
what? There was a rainbow!

Sally let me ride ahead with Lydia so I could get a shot of all the girls trotting up the lane with the rainbow arching up behind them. She even let me film without having to dismount because Amber was so calm and stood so still. Then she said she'd take some footage of me and Kayla doing something, so there would be some shots of us two together (Jody must have mentioned that to her too).

As we turned into the next field, there was a track going uphill, so me and Kayla hung back with Lydia while the other girls trotted to the top with Sally. Then Sally filmed us cantering up together. It was so much fun – we were neck and neck, racing each other, with Lydia behind. Even though Amber tried her best, Cracker's so speedy that they beat us! All the girls cheered when we reached the top and Sally said how good it was going to look in the film.

We had a canter up the next hill all together and that was great fun too – though of course me and Kayla had to go much slower that time because we were part of a bigger group.

On the way back, the rain came pelting down again and we were getting so wet that Sally let us stay in trot all the way back down the lanes and on to the yard, instead of going into walk. We were all squealing and giggling as we led our ponies into the barn.

After we'd changed and towelled down our hair in our rooms we had honey toast and hot blackcurrant round the kitchen table to warm up – yum!

We're having a disco tonight, and everyone's already talking about what they're going to wear. Genevieve's doing our hair because she's really good at it. She's got a huge washbag full of clips and bands and even her own curling tongs!

Friday morning, in bed!

I've woken up really early – Millie and Kayla are still asleep. I can't believe this is our last day here! I'm going to make sure I enjoy every second of it, and make the biggest fuss of Amber possible!

The disco last night was so cool, we all looked really grown up after Genevieve had done our hair and let us borrow her sparkly eyeshadow. I thought it would just be the curtains closed and some of Jody's CDs, but James actually has a proper mobile disco, with lights and everything!

We all danced loads and when this Rihanna song came on, me and Kayla did our routine to it that we made up at home. Yes – we actually did it in front of everyone. We really blushed when we realized Jody had filmed us with my camera, but when I played it back at bedtime, we looked OK!

There was karaoke too, and Sarah, Genevieve and Shanika sang a few songs together (they were fab and looked like a proper girl band!). Me, Kayla and Millie tried to do one too, but we

Disco pony!

were giggling so much we couldn't carry on. We ended up collapsing on the floor in hysterics, and Jas, Lexy and Ava had to take over! It was SO much fun – I just wish Amber could have been there!

I'm really looking forward to the gymkhana today – it's great that Mum and Dad are coming to see us, and Kayla's mum, too. I hope me and Amber win something – it would be brilliant to have a rosette to take home!

Oh, Millie's alarm's just gone off – time to get ready and fetch Amber from the field. Yippee! I can't wait to see her!

Sunnyside Stables

Friday, back at home
I just want to finish off this diary
before I forget anything!

This morning we had our final lesson (sob sob!) and then after a break for juice and biccies we started to get our ponies ready for the gymkhana. The sun was out again so we tied them up in the yard and got busy brushing and hoof-picking and plaiting. Everyone worked really hard and all the ponies looked fab.

When I'd finished, Amber looked so smart, like a show pony:

Shiny coat

plaits in the mane

matching ribbons on brow band

tail plaits with ribbons

hoof glitter

After lunch the parents started arriving, and we had to pack our stuff and take it down into the porch ready to go home (boo hoo!), but we also got changed into our smart gear for the gymkhana (hooray!). I got Genevieve to do my hair in a French plait to match Amber's tail and then Ava wanted the same as me so she did hers too.

We were standing in the kitchen all ready to go down to the yard when Mum and Dad walked in! It was so great to see them – I hadn't realized how much I'd missed them until that moment. Kayla was the same with her mum, too! When we went out on to the yard I took them to meet Amber and they both gave her a big pat and said how gorgeous she was. I managed to get a few shots of the girls doing their final brush downs and tacking up

before I had to hand the camera over to Dad
and get ready myself.

Mum, Dad and Kayla's mum stood with the
other parents by the manège
fence as we all filed in for the
tack and turn-out competition,
and I could see Dad filming us.
Ava and Star won, and Sarah
and Charm came second, so no
rosettes for me and Kayla, but never mind.
I just thought to myself, right I really *have* to
win a gymkhana race now!

Group B had their races first, so my group
rode out of the manège, dismounted and
stood by the fence watching, while our ponies
munched on the grass verge. Kayla looked
surprised and pleased when Sarah chose *her* to
be her relay partner — obviously she thought
Cracker would be really nippy — and she was
right, because they won!

I cheered for Kayla during the relay and apple bobbing. And I gave her an especially massive cheer when they won the cones race – Cracker's so quick at turning, he whizzed round the cones much faster than the others!

When it was our turn to do some races, I was so nervous and excited that my heart was hammering and my stomach was flipping over and over. It was really fun and guess what?! Me and Amber won a race too – the ball and bucket, where you had to pull up right by the bucket and throw the ball in (so all that practice we did in lessons of halting exactly at the markers really paid off!). Amber went from canter to halt in about two steps and our ball dropped straight in – unlike Jasmine's! (Sugar got a bit over-enthusiastic and went cantering straight past the bucket – twice!)

When we got our rosettes, all the parents
and Sunnyside staff gave us a big
cheer. As we walked our ponies
back into the barn, Kayla said,
"Thanks for encouraging me to stay
in Group B, Amy. That walk to
canter we learned really swung it for us
in the relay."

"No problem," I said, grinning. Then we had
a big hug.

When we'd sorted out our ponies (all taking
as long as possible!) we went into the games
room for tea and juice and biccies, and Jody
told all the parents about the video for the
website and got them to sign consent forms to
say we could be in it. Of course, as soon as
everyone's parents heard about it, they all
wanted to see it, even though I told them it
wasn't edited yet!

So we put the TV on in the games room and

plugged the camera in, and soon everyone was
glued to the screen. When it got to the
bit where Kayla falls in the poo

ha ha ha!

they all laughed and clapped
and called her a good sport.
"Don't worry, I'll take that out
in the edit," I promised her.
"No, don't," she said, "it's
really funny!"

It was so nice when everyone gave me a clap
at the end and said how well I'd done, making
the film – although I insisted it was pure fun and
not hard work at all!

After that it was definitely, absolutely time to
go home – we all thanked Jody and Sally and
Lydia and gave them big hugs (and Sarah and
Genevieve even hugged James while giggling a
lot!). Then came the hard part – going down to
the barn one last time to say goodbye to the
ponies. I gave Amber the biggest hug of all and

told her what a star she is. I know I'll miss her so much, but at least I've got loads of film of her and I can watch it every day.

As Kayla and I linked arms and walked across the lane to the car, we agreed that we've had the best holiday ever and that our ups and downs have only made our friendship stronger. And we're definitely coming back next summer! Right, Dad's going to help me edit the video now so I can get it over to Jody – I can't wait to see it up on the website!

Amy X

Collect all the books in the series!

  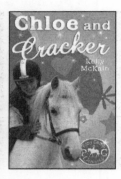

 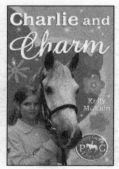

Collect all the books in the series!

Coming Soon:

Daisy and Dancer

Kelly McKain

Pony Camp Diaries

Daisy is thrilled to be at Pony Camp, where she teams up with gorgeous pony Dancer and quickly makes friends with her room-mates, twins Rosie and Isabel. When their instructor Sally takes them to see her friend perform a daring riding display, the girls are inspired to create their own. Rosie and Isabel are keen gymnasts and come up with a complex acrobatic routine for the three to perform at Friday's barbecue party. Daisy is desperate not to let her friends down, but she struggles — especially as Dancer spooks at everything too! Can Daisy and Dancer form a brilliant partnership in time to wow the crowd?

For all you fab Pony Camps fans, with love xxx

With special thanks to our cover stars,
Chloe and Nutmeg, and our brill
photographer, Zoe Cannon.

For loads of pony chat, visit:
www.kellymckain.co.uk

www.mandystanley.com

STRIPES PUBLISHING
An imprint of Magi Publications
1 The Coda Centre, 189 Munster Road, London SW6 6AW

A paperback original
First published in Great Britain in 2011

Text copyright © Kelly McKain, 2011
Illustrations copyright © Mandy Stanley, 2011
Cover photograph copyright © Zoe Cannon, 2011

ISBN: 978-1-84715-159-9

A CIP catalogue record for this book is available from the British Library.

Printed in the UK

2 4 6 8 10 9 7 5 3 1